Ulma, The Kidnapped Tree

Story and Illustrations by William J. Dalziel

This is a true story about a young Elm tree and her journey.

Dalziel's story of "Ulma, The Kidnapped Tree" tells us of an architect's dream in bringing an Elm tree, an American Liberty Tree, from Virginia to a shopping center in Southern California. This heart-filled story of a young Elm tree and her friend Charlie the Eastern Blue Jay, takes us on a journey of love and loss, sadness and freedom, and the trauma of an earthquake that eventually brings freedom to Ulma, The Liberty Tree.

This display type was set in Adobe Caslon Pro.
The text was set in 36 point Adobe Caslon Pro.
The art was created using Windsor Newton watercolor, pen & ink and digital media.
Designed & Edited by Diane L. Stevenett

This Book is Dedicated to

Daughters
Shenoah Rose & Shaelyn Audrey
for their encouragement, proof-reading & understanding.

& Granddaughters
Remy Laurel and Jolie Sage
for being so recently from God.

~ WJD

Throughout the cold eastern Winter, Ulma had been dreaming of her ancestors. Her family was called the "Liberty Tree", the symbol of this country's strength.

It was the beginning of Spring, and Ulma was just waking up from a long, cold Winter's sleep. Bright, fresh green leaves were already sprouting out of the ends of her fingers. She had been hybernating like a young bear.

She felt the wind wave her branches. The sun began to climb high above the bright, green treetops, above the surrounding forest.

The sun warmed her branches until tiny, new buds popped open like yellow popcorn, revealing small yellow flowers.

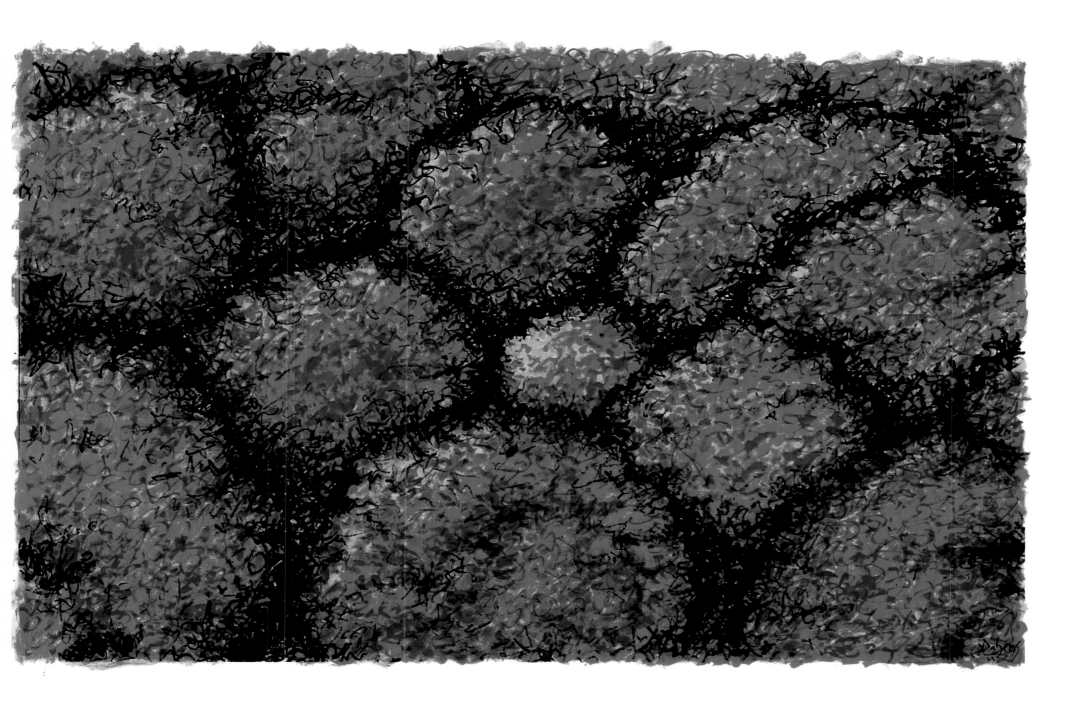

Charlie the resident Blue Jay, was up early poking some treasure he had probably stolen, into one of Ulma's diamond-shaped hiding places.

Ulma's wrinkles had become his Treasure Island.

Ulma was a perfect, young, symetrical tree.

That's when Ulma felt the ground shake...
and heard the sound of angry beasts coming
through the forest.

The vibrations grew stonger.

The sounds grew louder.

They were getting nearer.

With a loud protest, Charlie squeezed into a
small crevice in Ulma's side.

Ulma could smell the fire in the growling machine as it moved closer to her.

Suddenly, all of Ulma's creepy, crawly, bug forest friends abandoned ship.

Her friends and family in the forest were shocked and tried to hide.

A sharp pain shot up Ulma's legs.

Her waterfeeders were being cut off.

A cold metal hand took hold of her at the waist and with a jerk, pulled Ulma from out of her home. Her birthplace, Mother Earth.

Ulma was placed into a large wooden box, lifted up and laid down on her side, on a flatbed of cold steel.

A large black veil was draped over her entire body, tightly wrapped in heavy ropes and chained down so as not a branch could move.

Charlie screamed to his bird buddies for help. Too late. There was only dim, dark, scary shadows. The noise became a stinky, smoky growl.

They were being kidnapped!

Charlie was cool about it. He broke open a stash of seeds and fruit he'd hidden in her side.

With his mouth full, he began explaining what he believed was happening to them, and that his real name was Alphe J. Locoma, and her real name was Ulmacease, an old Aborigine family of the northern hemisphere.

Ulma couldn't understand a word he was saying, but she was very, very frightened.

The bumping up and down and sideways under a black tarp, surrounded by a constant roaring monster, and a wind that never let up, that smelled of fire and smoke, went on for days.

Charlie was hopping around in Ulma's tangled arms, trying to amuse her. He would screech, "I'm really a CROW you KNOW! I'm really a CROW you KNOW!"

He started calling himself Dr. J, Alphe, Chuck... and that he was actually a Professor of Poetry and Science. He was getting a tummy ache from snacking on all his hidden treats, telling one story after the next, each one a more fantastic lie than the next.

They finally shuddered to a stop. The veil of black and the heavy chains were pulled off.

Charlie hugged Ulma tightly and told her the future was bright, and that she would be OK. With a loud screech, he flew wildly up into the blinding sunlight and disappeared.

A bright blue sky shone above. Still in shock, Ulma was pulled upright. She took a deep breath and shook her branches free. Ulma was lifted up into the sky, and then down into a big, black hole... her new home.

Her long legs felt the enriched, moist soil.

Her growth slowed.
Her thoughts slowed.
The seasons never changed.
The air and temperature stayed the same.
The air was artificially chilled.

Between Summer and Winter, between Heaven and Earth, Ulma's days were always the same, lonely.

She missed Charlie the most, his screeches, his happy talk, his lies, his unbelievable stories. His poking at her skin felt like scratching an old itch.

Ulma stretched up, standing in a marble box. She could feel the cold, polished stone that surrounded her... a living monument in a large, bright, shiny room with glistening floors and sparkling lights. She heard the clicking sounds of plastic skylights being installed above her.

Ulma stood still in the middle of the room.
The sunlight was always on.
There was no breeze.
The nights became days.
People and animals walked and talked under and around her.

Then, early one morning, the shiny floors shuddered and the walls shook. There was dust like fog. It was hard for Ulma to breathe. The plastic ceiling fell in and broke into tiny pieces.

The big room that had held Ulma captive had fallen down. Only the morning sun surrounded her, and the brightness filled her branches. Ulma felt free.

Then in the silence, as the dust settled, Ulma heard a familiar scream that could only be ...Charlie!

As Charlie flew madly into her branches, he screamed, "ULMA!"

"Wake up! Wake up! You're dreaming!"

"It's SPRINGTIME!"

Ulma woke up! She could feel the warmth of the sun as it was making her branches and leaves grow. Ulma started telling Charlie her dream, but he had dozed off.

That's when Ulma felt the ground shake...

...and heard the sound of angry beasts coming through the forest.

And THAT is JUST the beginning of the story...

The Elm tree is a native of the North American hemisphere, and has lived on the East Coast from Newfoundland to Florida.

Their bark is like diamond-shaped fissures. They carry over one million leaves and have yellow drooping clusters of flowers in Spring. The Elm tree's seed is a light green wafer that drifts in the air like a kite. The Elm is known to have more strength than an Oak.

The Dutch Elm disease, a micro fungus, is one of its most feared diseases. It has killed almost ALL of the Elm trees in America.

The Elm has been called the *Liberty Tree*, meaning *the freedom of oppression.*

Shortly before the San Fernando, California earthquake of 1971, contractor & builder Bill Dalziel was hired as the Northridge Fashion Center Project Architect. The Bullock, Sears, JCPenney and Broadway tenants decided they wanted a live tree to be showcased in the center of the mall.

After researching the best trees, Bill decided on the sturdy Elm tree of the East Coast. He liked that the Elm has been called the *Liberty Tree*, meaning *the freedom of oppression.*

Bill travelled to a Virginia tree farm and chose one of the most-beautiful and healthiest of trees, then arranged for it to be transported to California.

This is a true story of a young Elm tree and her journey.

William "Bill" Dalziel was born at the Lansing College Hospital on the campus of Michigan State. He grew up in Michigan, leaving at the age of 19 for Art Center School of Design in Los Angeles, CA where he studied Architecture, Industrial/Auto design, Graphics, Painting and Illustration. He left for the military in 1955 to Paris Island at Camp Lejuenne, NC and then to Camp Pendleton, El Toro Marine Base, CA. as a liason between the US Marine Corp and the US Navy.

Dalziel, considered an *Abstract Expressionist* from the early 1960's, evokes feelings of strength and passion. His paintings are vibrant in color and depth, his language romantic, tender and direct. His bold geometric shapes evolve into intense coloration and sharply formed edges.

The author and artist's enthusiasm for creativity, life and the environment are communicated through his heart-filled stories, resonating poetry and, continually weaving intense color in word and paint, and multi-layers of line and shape. While living in Montectio, his *Sandbox Productions* TV Series hosted lively conversations with theologians, scientists, bankers, and more.

Bill Dalziel has traveled from New York to Paris on the Concorde, sailed across the Pacific to Honolulu with a K50 Kettemburg sloop, and visited Italy, Rome, Spain, Germany, Russia and Panama. A few of his lifetime influences include Escher, Buckminster Fuller, Mies Van der Rohe and The Bauhaus, Rumi, Hermann Hesse, Leonard Cohen, Akira Kurosawa, Toshiro Mifune, Eric Satie, John Cassavetes, Marlon Brando and Sam Peckinpah.

Currently, Bill Dalziel is producing a book of his poetry, **Zen Poetry and Musings** and his **Book Of Portraits**, to be released late fall of 2019.

If you're doing what you're supposed to be doing,
all the little stuff will be taken care of...including your rent."
~ *Bucky Fuller*